Farm Animals of Presidents

Grace Hansen

abdobooks.com

Published by Abdo Kids, a division of ABDO, P.O. Box 398166, Minneapolis, Minnesota 55439.
Copyright © 2022 by Abdo Consulting Group, Inc. International copyrights reserved in all countries.
No part of this book may be reproduced in any form without written permission from the publisher.
Abdo Kids Junior™ is a trademark and logo of Abdo Kids.

Printed in the United States of America, North Mankato, Minnesota.

102021
012022

THIS BOOK CONTAINS
RECYCLED MATERIALS

Photo Credits: Library of Congress, Shutterstock

Production Contributors: Teddy Borth, Jennie Forsberg, Grace Hansen

Design Contributors: Candice Keimig, Pakou Moua

Library of Congress Control Number: 2021939928
Publisher's Cataloging-in-Publication Data

Names: Hansen, Grace, author.

Title: Farm animals of presidents / by Grace Hansen

Description: Minneapolis, Minnesota : Abdo Kids, 2022 | Series: Pets of presidents | Includes online
resources and index.

Identifiers: ISBN 9781098209261 (lib. bdg.) | ISBN 9781644946916 (pbk.) | ISBN 9781098209964 (ebook)
| ISBN 9781098260323 (Read-to-Me ebook)

Subjects: LCSH: Livestock--Juvenile literature. | Pets--Juvenile literature. | Presidents--Juvenile literature. |
Presidents' pets--United States--Juvenile literature.

Classification: DDC 973--dc23

Table of Contents

Farm Animals of Presidents

Almost every US president has had pets. Some have even had farm animals!

William H. Harrison had
a cow named Sukey. It was
very normal to have a family
cow at the time.

William H.
Harrison
7

Lincoln had goats, Nanny and Nanko. They pulled Lincoln's sons around the White House!

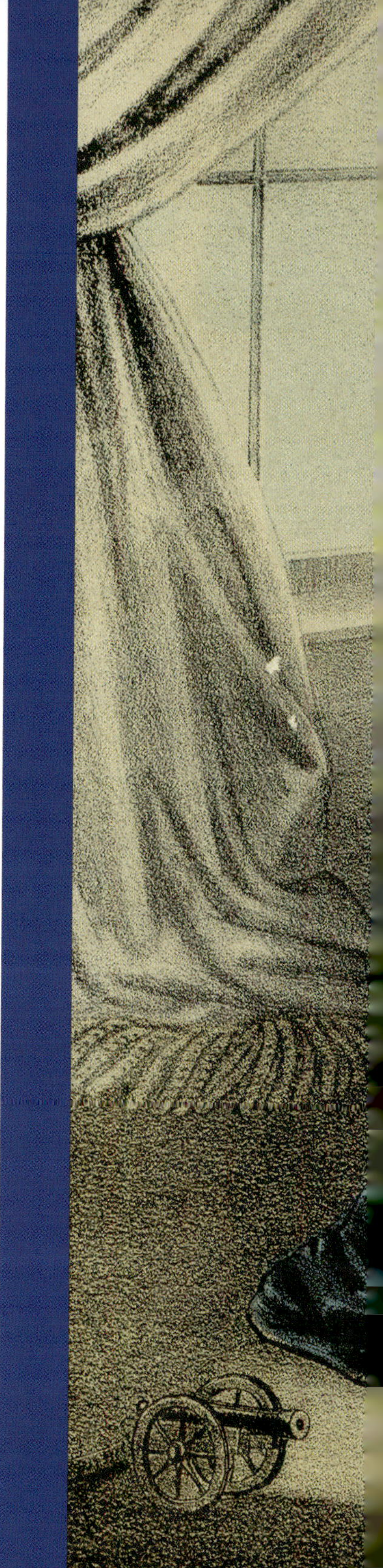

The Lincolns

Grover Cleveland had chickens. They lived in **stables** near the White House.

Grover
Cleveland

Benjamin Harrison also had
a pet goat. It was for his
grandchildren. Its name was
Old Whiskers.

Benjamin's son, Russel
Benjamin Harrison
13

William McKinley kept
roosters. No one is quite
sure how many.

15

William Taft was president until 1913. His cows were the last to live at the White House.

William
Taft
17

Woodrow Wilson had a flock of sheep. In 1919, he sold their wool for $52,823. He gave the money to the **Red Cross**.

Woodrow
Wilson

The Coolidges had many pets. One was a donkey named Ebenezer!

20

Calvin
Coolidge

More First Pets

George Washington
mules

Rutherford B. Hayes
cows

Theodore Roosevelt
Maude the pig

Woodrow Wilson
Old Ike the ram

Glossary

Red Cross
an organization that helps people who are living through wars or natural disasters.

stable
a building where animals are kept and fed.

Index

Visit **abdokids.com** to access crafts, games, videos, and more!